NEW WRITING AND WRITERS 20

Previously published

NEW WRITERS 1
Alan Burns, Monique Lange, Dino Buzzati
NEW WRITERS 2
Simon Vestdijk, Miodrag Bulatovic, Robert Pinget, Keith Johnstone
NEW WRITERS 3
Alexander Trocchi, Nick Rawson, Sinclair Beiles, David Mercer
NEW WRITERS 4 *Happenings*
Jean-Jaques Lebel, E.C. Nimmo, Charles Marowitz, Alan Kaprow, René de Obaldia, John Antrobus, Ken Dewey
NEW WRITERS 5
Daniel Castelain, Nazli Nour, Alex Neish
NEW WRITERS 6
Carol Burns, Penelope Shuttle, J.A. Dooley
NEW WRITERS 7
Tina Morris, Edmund Crackenedge, Kanwal Sundar
NEW WRITERS 8
Christine Bowler, Lyman Andrews, F.W. Willets
NEW WRITERS 9
Renate Rasp, Amanda Smyth, John Donovan
NEW WRITERS 10
Floyd Salas, Gerald Robitaille, Earl M. Coleman
NEW WRITERS 11
Svend Age Mardsen, David Mowat, J.M. Henegan
NEW WRITERS 12
David Galloway, Patrick Morrissey, Joyce Mansour
NEW WRITING AND WRITERS 13
Samuel Beckett, Steven Berkoff, Nikolai Bokov, Edward Bond, Elspeth Davie, Tony Duvert, A.R. Lamb, Gertrud Leutenegger, Naomi May, George Moor, N.E. Nikto, Antonia Pozzi, Roderick Watson
NEW WRITING AND WRITERS 14
Ingeborg Bachmann, Ann Benedek, Nikolai Bokov, Edward Bond, Pierre Bourgeade, Dino Buzzati, Peter French, Sadegh Hedayat, P.J. Kavanagh, René de Obaldia, Peter-Paul Zahl
NEW WRITING AND WRITERS 15
Heinrich Böll, Alan Brown, Michael Horovitz, P.J. Kavanagh, Jessie Kesson
NEW WRITING AND WRITERS 16
William Burroughs, Dino Buzzati, David Craig, Elspeth Davie, Ingeborg Drewitz, Kathleen Greenwood, Maryon Jeane, Neil Jordan, Sarah Lawson, B.C. Leale, Sarah McCoy, Michael Moorcock
NEW WRITING AND WRITERS 17
Samuel Beckett, Nikolai Bokov, Jan Cremer, Harry Mulisch, Yves Navarre, Robert Pinget, John Wynne
NEW WRITING AND WRITERS 18
Yves Bonnefoy, Copi, A.R. Lamb, B.C. Leale, Harry Mulisch, Naiwu Osahon, Calum Ross, Tibor Várady
NEW WRITING AND WRITERS 19
Edward Bond, Copi, Patrick Morrissey, Harry Mulisch, Martin Walser

NEW WRITING AND WRITERS 20

by

Samuel Beckett, Nikolai Bokov, Pat Connolly,
Sorel Etrog, George Moor

JOHN CALDER · LONDON
RIVERRUN PRESS · NEW YORK

This edition first published 1983 in Great Britain by
John Calder (Publishers) Limited,
18 Brewer Street, London W1R 4AS
and first published 1983 in the USA by
Riverrun Press Inc.,
175 Fifth Avenue, New York, NY 10010

THE MYSTERY OF THE KINGFISHER BOX © George Moor 1982, 1983
ONE EVENING © Samuel Beckett 1980, 1982, 1983
Originally published in Journal of Beckett Studies, No. 6, Autumn 1980.
WE ARE FLYING OVER THE VALLEY © Nikolai Bokov 1982, 1983
Translation © Sophie Lund, 1982, 1983
HINGES © Sorel Etrog 1982
MARKS, GAPS, DEATH CAR © Pat Connolly 1982, 1983

ALL RIGHTS RESERVED

The publishers gratefully acknowledge financial assistance from the Arts Council of Great Britain.

British Library Cataloguing in Publication Data

New Writing and writers.—20
  1. English literature—20th century—
     Periodicals
  820'.8'00912   PR 1148

ISBN 0 7145 3869 8 paperback

Any paperback edition of this book whether published simultaneously with, or subsequent to, the hardback edition is sold subject to the condition that it shall not, by way of trade, be lent, resold, hired out, or otherwise disposed of, without the publishers' consent, in any form of cover other than that in which it is published.

No part of this publication may be reproduced, stored in a retrieval system, or transmitted in any form by any means, electronic, mechanical, recording or otherwise, except brief extracts for the purpose of review, without the prior written permission of the copyright owner and publishers.

Photoset in North Wales in 11/11 Baskerville by Derek Doyle and Associates, High Street, Mold. Printed and bound in Great Britain at The Camelot Press Ltd, Southampton.

CONTENTS

	Page
INTRODUCTION	xi

Samuel Beckett
ONE EVENING   13

Nikolai Bokov
WE ARE FLYING OVER THE VALLEY   17

Pat Connolly
Three Stories: 33
MARKS   35
GAPS   39
DEATH CAR   41

Sorel Etrog
HINGES   45

George Moor
THE MYSTERY OF THE KINGFISHER BOX   1

ACKNOWLEDGEMENTS

ONE EVENING by Samuel Beckett was first published in
Journal of Beckett Studies, No. 6, Autumn 1980.

INTRODUCTION

INTRODUCTION

The twentieth *NWW* contains work from six authors, three of whom have appeared before in the series and three new to it. The short text from Samuel Beckett, who has always been generous in contributing short work to the series, has appeared once before and will only be known to the specialized readership of the *Journal of Beckett Studies*. It is a beautifully evocative text redolent of the stillness that typifies his recent work with much compressed imagery. George Moor, whose *The Heat of the Sun* received much favourable comment from the critics when first published in *NWW 13*, has, in *The Secret of the Kingfisher Box*, written a novel that combines the technique of mystery fiction in an English country setting with a strange oriental menace that leads to the denouement. Nikolai Bokov, a Russian émigré now living in Paris, has also been published in several issues of this series, and like Mr Beckett and Mr Moor is on the Calder fiction list. The poetic text contained here shows a movement away from his earlier satirical writing towards impressionistic observation.

Among the newcomers Pat Connolly was brought up in England, now lives in New York, and has written some unusual short stories of real quality with an original approach to descriptions of people and places. Sorel Etrog was born in Rumania, lives mostly in Toronto, but also has studios in various European capitals. As sculptor and painter he has a world reputation, but has recently also written, designed and directed for the theatre; *Hinges* reveals an unusual approach, Dada-influenced and very complex.

A recent article in *The Sunday Times* (London) claimed that quality fiction is doing better, citing four books that have had unusually large paperback sales. But two of their authors have been established for well over twenty years and one of the other two must thank American commercial hype for his belated British success, so this welcome but untypical statement must not be taken too seriously. The conclusion to be drawn is that the British publishing scene is ever more rapidly following the American in highlighting a few books or authors every year that everyone wants to read while all the other offerings are largely ignored by both press and public. *NWW* continues to do what it can to encourage wider rather than narrower literary interest by giving a platform to established work of uneconomic lengths and to writers who have something new to say or a new way to say it.

The Publishers

I
ONE EVENING

Samuel Beckett

Translated from the French by the author

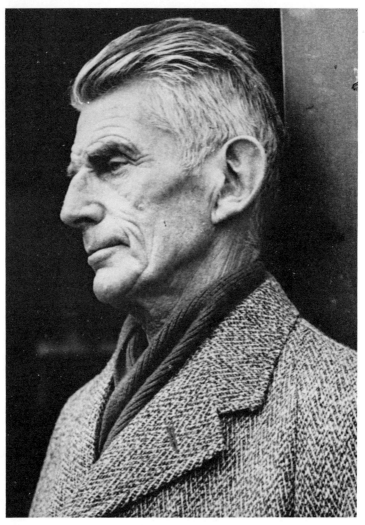

Photograph by Jerry Bauer

Samuel Beckett's international reputation began with the world wide success of his play *Waiting for Godot*. He has since written many plays and novels which have made him the most discussed and academically studied post-war writer. He was awarded the Nobel Prize for Literature in 1969. His most recent publications are *Company* and *Ill Seen Ill Said* (John Calder). He lives in France and writes in both English and French, translating himself from one language to the other.

ONE EVENING

He was found lying on the ground. No one had missed him. No one was looking for him. An old woman found him. To put it vaguely. It happened so long ago. She was straying in search of wild flowers. Yellow only. With no eyes but for these she stumbled on him lying there. He lay face downward and arms outspread. He wore a greatcoat in spite of the time of year. Hidden by the body a long row of buttons fastened it all the way down. Buttons of all shapes and sizes. Worn upright the skirts swept the ground. That seems to hang together. Near the head a hat lay askew on the ground. At once on its brim and crown. He lay inconspicuous in the greenish coat. To catch an eye searching from afar there was only the white head. May she have seen him somewhere before? Somewhere on his feet before? Not too fast. She was all in black. The hem of her long black skirt trailed in the grass. It was close of day. Should she now move away into the east her shadow would go before. A long black shadow. It was lambing time. But there were no lambs. She could see none. Were a third party to chance that way theirs were the only bodies he would see. First that of the old woman standing. Then on drawing near it lying on the ground. That seems to hang together. The deserted fields. The old woman all in black stockstill. The body stockstill on the ground. Yellow at the end of the black arm. The white hair in the grass. The east foundering in night. Not too fast. The weather. Sky overcast all day till evening. In the west-north-west near the verge already the sun came out at last. Rain? A few drops if you will. A few drops in the morning if you will. In the present to conclude. It happened so long ago. Cooped indoors all day she comes out with the sun. She makes haste to gain the fields. Surprised to have seen no one on the way she strays feverishly in search of the wild flowers. Feverishly seeing the imminence of night. She remarks with surprise the absence of lambs in great numbers here at this time of year. She is wearing the black she took on when widowed young. It is to reflower the grave she strays in search of the flowers he had loved. But for the need of yellow at the end of the black arm there would be none. There are therefore only as few as possible. This is for her the third surprise since she came out. For they grow in plenty here at this time of year. Her old friend her shadow irks her. So much so that she turns to face the sun. Any flower wide of her course she reaches sidelong. She craves for sundown to end and to stray freely again in the long afterglow. Further to her distress the familiar rustle of her long black skirt in the grass. She moves with half-closed eyes as if drawn on into the glare. She may say to herself it is too much strangeness for a single March or April evening. No one abroad. Not a single lamb. Scarcely a flower. Shadow and rustle irksome. And to crown all the shock of her foot against a body. Chance. No one had missed him. No one was looking for him. Black and green of the garments touching now. Near the white head the yellow of the few plucked flowers. The old sunlit face. Tableau vivant if you will. In its way. All is silent from now on. For as long as she cannot move. The sun disappears at last and with it all shadow. All shadow here. Slow fade of afterglow. Night without moon or stars. All that seems to hang together. But no more about it.

II
WE ARE FLYING OVER THE VALLEY

Nikolai Bokov

Translated by Sophie Lund

Photograph by Jerry Bauer

Nikolai Bokov is a Russian emigré writer, now 35 years old. He left the Soviet Union in 1975 and has since lived in Paris. His novel *Nobody*, which was distributed as a *samizdat* text in Russia, was published anonymously in Britain in 1975 (John Calder), and subsequently his short stories have appeared in *New Writing and Writers 13, 14* and *17*.

WE ARE FLYING OVER THE VALLEY

Black dot: the black hole of a revolver's barrel. Faced by this degree of foreshortening, even an expert will need time to determine the make of a gun. The dead fist gripped the butt of the revolver: painted, almost real, the isolated fist held the gun, aiming at him through the shop window. It would appear that the gunsmith was no stranger to art, and appreciated rules — at any rate where they related to beauty, which on occasion does have a profound effect.

Tearing his gaze away with difficulty, he now perceived something different: the face of the passer-by who was standing beside him, the face of a woman in fact, and dark in the glass, as if the day were not sunlit and transparent. And through the face, he saw the navy blue covering of the display shelves in the window, and the interiors of the guncases, blood-stained in advance, from which the weapons peered: capable of halting a running man, catching him in mid-leap, interrupting his stroll, his lonely reverie, to say nothing of his flight.

He saw a smile. His reflection smiled back at hers. They did not turn towards each other, trying in this way, it would seem, to avoid the ignominy of a street encounter, for which there can never be any excuse — Well, not unless a preordained second meeting should occur of its own accord, or one of the parties be employed at some public institution where anyone might wander in quite naturally, or unless, let us say, she'd been stuck in a lift and he had come to her rescue.

'What's caught your eye in there?'
'Who me? What? Well, that little velvet cushion, as a matter of fact ...'
(A superb long-barrelled colt reposed upon it).
'Velvet? But it's paper!'

And he felt vexed, as if reality was now to contain yet another prosaic detail, but then isn't reality made up of details anyway? If every one of these details were suddenly — through his hastiness — to turn into paper, what would become of reality itself? How simple it would be to strike a match and to watch as the page became charred at its edges, turned itself into a suffocating little tube, destroying if not everything, then at any rate the middle, the end, and as in the present circumstances, the beginning. But, be that as it may, there is a little something to reality — there is fire, for instance, or water.

Having drunk the water, he stayed with the glass in his hand. It's so easy to sift through the fragments of your life, without any intention, incidentally, of putting them on public view, and just occasionally to make a hitherto non existent picture emerge. There were times when he would breast the last row of hillocks, laden with grape vines and grapes, the fruit covered in dust, some with crusty sides, others which had even cracked open (how the wasps swarmed above them!), and see the deserted shore, where there was no one, no one — just a black speck over there, a dog in all probability, judging from the speed at which it moved. The strong wind of the region carried it closer to the oncoming wave, and he would follow the black speck with his eyes as it zigzagged to and fro.

Or, hardly out of the sea, he'd feel the heat under his feet, soon the sand would begin to burn — after he had taken his twenty-first step, according to a calculation which dated from the time when he used to amuse himself with science. But the palm of his hand would be cold still: he'd touch the hot skin of her shoulder, brushing over the shoulder blades, and a little trail of goose pimples would run like lightning down her back, rounding her thighs before disappearing, anticipating the movement of the hand, premonition and guide at one and the same time. The hand, already hot, sets off in pursuit.

Or: how is living, mortal man to avoid that day when he sees a face, absolutely still, no longer able to come close, lips which can no longer speak a single word, not even the name of one who was dear, a friend, or simply pleasing, a companion. What is this? Fear, or pity, or parting? Not yet

— after all the body lies there, very close, people still sob aloud or just weep soundlessly. And when the parting does come, oh, the hope for a reunion in another existence: has my touch really had its fill of your hair, your cheeks, your shoulders, your thighs ... and even your toes? And have my lips really followed the night long path of my hands, and has the honey of kisses really melted all away? But there comes a dawn with a different face: flowers at the bedhead, their scent mingling with another dangerous, frightening, scent — faint no longer, already heavy, edging out the air.

And are these the components of a picture? A deserted shore, the two of them, and death which waits for the setting of the sun. If you put these fragments together — they will merge into each other — how can such a picture not be realized? All that remained would be a little table in a café, in a dimly lit corner, a glass, perhaps, of beer, and the mighty neck of the proprietor: he sees me as a feature of the décor. He is Russian, he says to one of his customers. Others turn round to have a look: scraps of the torn page float in the air, together with the death which has not happened — and they do too.

Their heads nod: the mighty purple neck, the other thin necks, so that is what they are like, the Russians, well, well ... that is what they are like. The scraps of torn paper sink slowly to the ground, fold themselves up: the shoreline curved like a bow, the hills, the waves. They are walking slowly along the edge of the sea, and if the shore does not come to an end, if there is time to add to it — working feverishly, oblivious to any word let alone gesture — they will go on walking, chatting to each other, or just with their hands touching, and he will see the living seaweed of her eyes, and never the cold reflection of clinical light, and the uninterested pupils. It's too much! Too much! screeches the head on the mighty neck: waiters mop up the customer, the glass of a beer mug crunches underfoot. Naturally, they won't let me extend the shoreline — and they are carefree, those two, stepping lightly on the sandy shore. A lunge forward: I could be in time, I could ... Too much! Hello! How's things! screeches the parrot, a feature of the décor. The scraps of paper fall one after the other, together with the parrot, the customers, with death: although not at once, they glide through the air. The sweet, cold, night air.

The day before: a layer of lipstick on her mouth, for the moment on her mouth, for the moment on her. She came too close to the mirror: in the mist suddenly obscuring her face, she could have seen only a small scarlet ring, a circle, almost a dot, almost an oblong scar. The man — curly headed ... just a moment, I can't quite see ... that's better ... curly headed, dark, sluggish — did not get up from the bed. He felt a burning sensation on his chest, coming from the surface of his skin, as if from a sting. 'It burns,' he said. 'What?' 'It burns.' 'Where?' She turned away from the mirror in such a way as to cause her unbuttoned blouse to fly up around her shoulders and appear quite black in the half light of the closed shutters. The burning sensation was below his left nipple, and she thought that she saw something there ... but then calmed down. 'It's all normal.' I think that it was exactly on this spot that yesterday, leaning over him, (she was trying to reach the cheese), she had dropped hot ash from her cigarette. 'It burns? Well, that's strange, isn't it. Never mind, it'll go away.' She kissed the place, and saw the imprint: almost a circle, just like a ring. It was because of the extra greasy layer of lipstick on her mouth that a trace appeared on his chest, just under his left nipple, or rather a little below, but not above — one, two — the fifth rib, counting, naturally, from the bottom. He put his clothes on reluctantly, listening with irritation to the sports news, and for some reason, to the rest of the news as well: petrol prices had jumped, and as for coffee, the least said the better. The Russians, as usual, wanted a lasting peace ... the experts insisted that this was so ... and in any case were still far away.

'We're off to see the gang', he said. She took a last look in the mirror — a fleeting, rapid, glance.

The car would not start for a long time. (This isn't true: they get into the car, the door almost slams on her dress, but no, it's all right. The engine starts immediately).

Elements we know well: fire, air, water, earth. In their pure form they are rarely present when death and love occur, which are themselves also elements, but, without our participation, of no interest to anyone save perhaps philosophers. Life presents of itself a mixture of elements in equal proportions, but should one prevail over the others,

We Are Flying Over the Valley

something great is born. For instance, a conflagration is fire prevailing. An ocean: water. Two figures stand high on a hill — a man and a woman, most likely in an embrace — high on that hill air holds dominion since, after all, in motion it becomes wind and causes the sleeves of the young woman's blouse to fill and billow. Obviously, there is earth too, underfoot — at any rate under their feet — but we are not concerned with it.

Observe well proportioned life: an appetizing dish bubbles on the fire, strong hands wash a thick neck under a jet of water. A fan turns. Love and death conform: a woman, full of energy, gazes despairingly at her husband's back, and at the same time glances with impatience at the telephone. A cat enters with a mouse in its teeth — probably it's a toy mouse made of rubber. Of course there can be no death here: these people are immortal.

There is one element which has not been mentioned, and this is unjust: it muddles all the others, changes them in places, its name is madness. It does not know love, hides it, forces you to see an instrument of death in a kiss, and transforms each gesture into danger. It is a powerful element, I tell myself as I walk down the stony path from the top of the hill: the deserted shore, the absence of any human being and, from the deserted sea, the road which stretches at the base of the pine trees, between the hillocks, towards the deserted little town. Steep cobbled streets, dusty café windows, a half opened door, and looking as if it has been newly washed, the window of the gun shop. The collar of an unbuttoned blouse is reflected in the glass. 'Do you like it?' 'Who me?' 'Look at that beautiful dagger — it comes from Spain.' The knife rested upon the velvet paper, a little apart, not very broad, but with an ornate handle and a distinctly visible narrow groove on the thick side of the blade. Childhood friends used to tell me that the groove was there to drain the blood. And for a long time I believed this explanation, until they laughed at me, those friends of my youth. It's the hard rib, they told me, which stops the knife from bending even when it meets bone, and enables it to d its work.

The half opened door of the café: the sound of a wafting through. 'Do you know that song? No? Why n rather like it.' He listens to the words. 'We're flying over t valley, where we were born, where we walked beside the stream, and loved, and died ... not so fast, don't fly over it so fast.'

'You have a strange accent. Are you from the south?' Am I from the south? From the north more like.

'From the north.'

'But you were born in the south?'

Where was I born? Must I remember? Isn't it enough that one is born at all on this earth, that, somewhere, one cries out for the first time — from fear of course, at the sight of all those yellow circles in the darkshifting mass, of that sun piercing the crown of the tree beneath the window.

'Well you know, you see ... I was, well I was a deaf mute. I began to speak, as it were, when I was thirty years old, and so probably ...'

'But you're much younger than thirty! I would never have thought you were thirty!'

He was already planning to develop this deaf and dumb theme.

'Incredible! I thought you were twenty — oh, say — twenty five at the most!'

Past the little hills, the vines — yellow and deserted on the red earth — along the stony, whitish road: they climb to the crest of the hill, and already only their silhouettes can be seen, as if they are climbing up to the sky, to the little cloud with a rosy rim. Navy blue wedges of evening shadow slice into the hillocks, the greenery is growing darker. The sea appears, and the islands: the distant ones scarcely defined against the fog which is drowning the area. There is no sound of birds, and only gusts of wind bring the sudden sound of waves: taut white long-bows advancing towards the shore. There is just a solitary black speck moving, probably a dog bowled along by the wind — it runs in zigzags.

With every step the sea grows louder — already there is the din of rollers beating against the breakwater. Night. Fog. Moon. The sharp silent flashing of the lighthouse. The ruins of a little summer shack — in all probability the kiosk of a newspaper vendor, or some other — but wait, ice creams were sold here, and cold drinks! Of course, that's **what it was — there's the head on the mighty neck raising**

We Are Flying Over the Valley

itself from the deckchair, the woman, not yet devoid of all attraction, in the next chair. Summer flesh under the awnings, radios, music, fruit, and the mighty neck supporting the sturdy head, folds hanging down from the body like some insignia of prosperity, the armour of wealth.

He buys an ice cream, a packet of nuts — almonds to begin with — and then peanuts, a can of Coca Cola, and six cans of beer. Pausing for thought, he adds a ham sandwich, a pâté sandwich, a little carton of cold meat salad, and some chocolate. Strong fingers undo the purse, take out a hundred franc note (bearing the portrait of Corneille), but then discover something smaller: fifty francs (with Voltaire: oh, philosopher of Ferney, can your wisdom really be exactly twice as cheap as literature?) The wife feigns sleep, hiding her face beneath a magazine: the cover shows Russians marching. She sees standing beside her a pair of hairy calves, her gaze travels upwards along the pale blue veins which stand out in abundance on the thighs, (that's the nature of the job, all your life on your feet, you understand, behind the counter), her gaze travels higher still to the pendulous belly: she pretends to be asleep. Meanwhile, a mountain of emerald blue water grows on the horizon, until those who are lying down can no longer see the sky. It crashes down on the sand, washing away bodies, garbage, disintegrating the wooden walls of the stall with a cracking sound, splintering the shards of broken boards, and in receding carries away a shoal of white sandwiches.

The ruins are covered in sand. Night. Fog. Moon. Lips whisper a name. The hot palm of a hand touches cheeks, hair: the face is paler than the surrounding night; he sees the lids twitch, suddenly laying bare the eyes: she would have seen the moon, or rather a pale blotch in the fog — perhaps she does — she sees his face.

Night. Fog. Moon. Buildings line the railway tracks, but they leave room enough for waste land: waste land. A man's silhouette beside the motor car, the little flame of a cigarette. Wires hang down like staves: you can just hear music. If you strain your ears, there is the rythmical crunch of gravel beneath the feet of an approaching man, even several men, and there where there are three of them with but a single thought, the footsteps take on the gait of a six-footed creature. It moves between the piles of gravel, the lone figure beside the motor car feels the tension of waiting, detaches itself from the car, becoming barely visible; the black patch has moved away from the pale patch of the motor car, and dissolved. They halted in a semi circle a short distance away, but the crunch of the gravel did not cease: skirting them from the side, a fourth man was coming towards him, a stranger, and yet there was something about the contour of the head that reminded him of someone he knew, and was waiting to meet that night.

He felt as if he had been stung on the breast, a sudden burning sensation, which having begun on the surface, was now penetrating deep inside. Last night, leaning against his stomach to sip wine out of a glass, she had spilled hot cigarette ash: music warmth, alcohol. The music of an old record, with the hum of a needle, the ash breaking off, falling, falling, burning: the place marked, and the burning sensation growing more and more acute with every step of the man who was coming, even to all intents and purposes, staggering slightly, towards him: the burn, starting at one point on his skin, and then penetrating deep was the reason why he did not feel it: the blow, as if something had snagged his ribs, bent the bone, and entered. There was only something hot, running down over his belly under his clothes, down into the groin and lower still, spilling over his naked legs, his feet which became numb immediately, and his toes — gathering between them, soaking the leather of his shoes, and the gravel, and the earth beneath them.

Night. Fog. Arms flung wide, a man motionless. The torn strap of a raincoat. The lamp aims its pools of light, the giant button shines.

It is too late to tear up the used page.

'I want to tell you something ... but you mustn't laugh, all right?

What exactly, he wondered. The seaside café was deserted. The proprietor stood behind the counter, wiry, with swift eyes which saw everything at once: a blouse, seemingly violet in colour, showed beneath the woman's jacket. A man in a peaked cap drew up in a rickety motor car and carried in a bundle: the newspapers.

What, exactly, does she want to tell me? Does she — he

We Are Flying Over the Valley

sipped his coffee, feeling the warmth flow downwards inside his body. Probably — it's not to be excluded — she'll tell me that she is married, and how sorry that makes her. That she is only going to be here for another day or two — three at the most. Four perhaps. No, it's unlikely to be four, two days at the very outside.

'But look, you aren't going to laugh are you?'

With what speed I gain this sort of reputation! — he said to himself. Everywhere and always, not without foundation of course, but it's getting to be too much. She leaned towards him, holding back the hair which cascaded down all the same, hiding her face, and he could just catch: 'I am happy ... with you.' He parted her hair, and met her gaze: it held an explanation, the reason why, and he could already read, as if he were deaf, those same words on the scarce moving lips. Her pink cheeks were lit by the sun: warmth spilled through the air, and the sun threw its rays further and higher: the shelves which held hundreds of bottles flared like a collar of northern lights, green and dark blue and ruby red, blood red — the colour of blood predominated on the shelves. The proprietor's face was yellow in the sunlight. He screwed up his eyes, a grimace of displeasure froze on his face for the remainder of the day.

Does he see that the man with the young woman is agitated, (is he happy or the reverse?) His forehead, cheeks, nose, have reddened: he uncurls the palm of her hand, and lays it against his face: the scent of waterside willow, bitter bark, damp grass — where does it come from? He breathes in the freshness of the cool palm, and the sounds of his native tongue fill his hearing, he even says something, and only then realizes that he has expressed himself awkwardly, that he is speaking an abracadabra — leafy maybe, ringleted, pleasant to the ear — from a far away corner of the earth where people have quite other pursuits, distinctly other — to be precise, they study the science of death and madness, where morning and evening gravel crunches beneath the feet of a six-footed, eight-footed, creature, a centipede, where it is always: Night. Moon. Wasteland.

Her hair covers his face: 'With you I am so, I don't know, do you understand ... you won't ...'

The jacket slipped from her shoulders and he could see them portrayed in the mist of the sun drenched blouse. He saw the face in the mist, and the white chairs on the terrace, beaded with dew. He pulled himself together, asked the proprietor for a newspaper, and unfolded it with deliberate slowness. *Morning.* In bold type: The Russians in Africa, and a photograph with a caption which said 'Russians Marching'. In smaller type: Squaring of accounts. In the vicinity of Debussy Parade ... identity not established ... lipstick ... according to police opinion, drug traffickers ...

The page of the newspaper bent back on itself. She was smoking another cigarette, gazing absent-mindedly at the photograph of the murdered man. And then he saw interest, and attentiveness, and a look of pain suddenly gripping her face.

Hello! It's too much! How's things! screeches the parrot, and at the same time whistles a little in surprise. This, of course, is not all the proprietor says — nearly, but not all. The parrot is in clover: the proprietor has gone to the bank, while his comely, still attractive wife is on the telephone, smiling an uncertain smile, as if listening to something agreeable, and as if she can be seen by her interlocuter. She is talking, without any doubt, to a man — playing with the salt cellar, the pepper and mustard pots which she has taken from their stand: forming a triangle out of these powerful seasonings, pepper, mustard, salt. Absent-mindedly, she pushes the untidy bulbous mustard pot to the side — so far to the side that it almost falls behind the counter. Pepper and salt are left: the well-groomed little fingers move them around, as if performing some strange dance, foretelling something, and then suddenly squeeze the neck of the pepper pot: the knuckles grow white. It's too much! Hello! How's things! screeches the parrot: the proprietor is away, he's at the bank, there are few customers. The parrot's conversational gifts are unrivalled.

But to this vaguely grubby café in the capital, I prefer the one in the far provinces: descending from the hill along the stony road, past the houses shut up until summer, past the trees which step further and further back from the sea. A grey day, wind, rain. Pieces of wood, washed white — heavy, naked — resemble the bones of some animal. In front, a dog runs in zigzags, bowled along by the wind, its paw prints are already blurred at the edges, half erased.

We Are Flying Over the Valley

Good morning, we say almost in unison, the proprietor and I. Hastily, he produces a cup of coffee: he is reading a fresh copy of *Morning*. I open the page. Her face, which yesterday morning was beside me, and the evening before, and the night, is now a different face: it shows sorrow, silence, peace, as if it belonged to a runner who has stopped running, and has had time to catch his breath. 'Last night ... made an appearance ... aware of the identity ... on Diu (misprint) bessy Parade ... 19 years of age, member of an engineer's family ...'

A penetrating gaze: the wiry proprietor studies the face of yesterday's customer, gathering himself, holding himself taut and at the ready, meeting the customer's eye: beads of sweat break out above the thick eyebrows, as if dispensed from a dropper beneath the skin, the proprietor is sweating, the words freeze upon lips which have turned blue: You were here yesterday, and so was she ...

He could say no: to the end, everywhere and at all times he would deny the night and the moon, the lips whispering his name, the heavy beat of the waves in the distance, and the earth shuddering beneath the assault of the water.

Yes. Along the road to the top of the hill, covered in crooked trees and bushes bearing berries the colour of dried blood.

Going out, he can already hear the whirr of the telephone dial, and begins to run through the sea shore scrub, his choice of route totally devoid of logic: he'll slip in the rain. Here and there, his wet clothing is wreathed in steam, he is gasping for breath. A car catches up with him on the rise to the highway: How do I get to ... I'll go with you, it's on my way, I'll show you.

He sees a face in the rear-view mirror: plastered hair, panting mouth, can that be him? It is.

A double row of slightly murky walls, with a narrow passage between them, half-filled by a broad back. Her face is far away, at a distance of two or three paces, and her voice is unrecognizable: a distorted telephone voice masked by a fine wire mesh. She kisses him — he sees the lips part a little, the lids close. He watches, pushing with his hands against the glass which nothing, not even a heavy calibre bullet, will puncture. 'My darling,' he hears, 'my darling, kiss me, come closer, touch me ... ' He kisses her, as if the transparent wall, with its black spot, a squashed dead fly, does not exist, and he hears: 'I don't know why, how ... tell me: didn't we stay together, just remind me ...'

Look: black cliffs, and the sea beneath them, and the waves which lose their strength and their shape upon the shore. The music of the reeds, bending like waves beneath the wind which fills your blouse — I see a triangle of sunburnt skin, smooth and shiny. Little snakes of sand slither round our feet, the faded sun sinks lower, clouds stand in a semi-circle, echoing the line of the shore. Further away, the dark green hills are etched against the dark blue sky, and the silhouettes of those walking along the stony white road merge when they reach the highest point, and even if you were to hurry after them, you would not reach them in time: night advances upon the hills, covering them in shadow, and only the moon lights the path — white, running with chalk, like a belt thrown in the thick grass, like arms flung wide — in the thick green grass.

The moon shines through the window: a gold earring glitters on the table, elongated like a drop of water flying through space, and the glitter of the gold is repeated by the shimmering skin, and the paths left by the moist palm which rounds a thigh, trembling, and the rapid pulsation of his blood in his swelling veins, and the breath which burns his face as if the air were on fire: as if their breathing filled the room, the hills and the valley ... my darling ... he hears: he cannot make out the face, hidden by the oval of misted glass, but he sees, rising from the depths, an expression almost of pain.

'Get it over!', the policeman says, bending towards his ear, but it's no use: the surge of manhood leaves him.

'Your visit is over.'

Two white patches: her hands, pressed to the transparent wall opposite, separated from his wall by the corridor. The broad back tears their gaze apart, the well cut uniform, the layers of muscle, but he manages to hear: my darling ...

'Allow me to express the hope that your influence will prove beneficial,' someone in nicely tailored civilian clothes tells him.

A sunny day. Absentmindedly, he buys a newspaper, unfolds it. The black patch of a headline: DEBUSSY. But

We Are Flying Over the Valley

no, it's nothing, nothing, some concert or other, nothing, nothing, it'll pass, it happens and then it passes, the main thing is to shut your eyes and not see, not hear, sit it out, nothing, nothing, nothing ...

It's completely unimportant who — who? — is guilty, whether it is she or others, but in fact he forgot to tell her so, has only just thought of it: I will always be on your side, together with the hills, the valley, the road, the moon, together with the warmth which comes from some unknown corner of the earth, with that drop of gold — he opens the palm of his hand: as if caught in flight, an elongated form pierces his skin with its sharp end: the gold earring, dulled by blood.

He notices another reader of newspapers leaning almost right up against the kiosk opposite the entrance to the railway station. A light coloured raincoat, belted with a leather belt. The forgotten feeling rises slowly within him. His muscles fill with strength. Walking lightly, he embarks on the circle of the approaching chase.

A far corner of the station lavatory. And the reader of newspapers, damn it, suddenly feels the need, but stops, goes no further. He, meanwhile, takes cover behind the little structure of the urinal, as if intending to go in, but then chooses another course of action: after all the decorative concrete fence is only a little taller than he is himself.

Street. Evening. He is alone.

The parrot's cage is covered by a black cloth: it's time, my friend, you've talked enough all this long day, for you night has come, as it has for us too: the time of the late drink, of unrealized meetings, of indolent imaginings. The mighty neck above the cash register: the proprietor is vague, gazing out like a Buddha. Further away, at the little tables, conversations are drawing to a close. The cold cigar clamped between the teeth of the customer standing in a somewhat picturesque pose at the counter. The lamb, frozen in its niche below the arch of the sign which says 'Restaurant', eyes glittering as if alive, but alas quite lifeless, stuffed, or worse still, a waxwork. Upon the mirror, the length and breadth of an entire wall, blooms an enormous bouquet, blooms one year, two, three, and longer: the painted artificial flowers have faded.

For a moment the street sounds grow louder: probably the door has opened, probably someone has come in. A woman's voice requests a glass of lemonade. Silence. The woman's voice repeats its request. The popping of a cork. The rattle of change. The click of the juke box, set in motion. The steel claw moves along the row of black discs. Slowly the needle begins its approach ... nearer and nearer to the edge of the shining black disc, nearer and nearer — I find I am even shaking, I am even ... Among the artificial flowers I see a dark head.

'We are flying over the valley ... we are flying over the valley ... we are flying ...'

III
THREE STORIES
Pat Connolly

Photograph by courtesy of Pat Connolly

Pat Connolly was born in London and spent her childhood in Berkshire. She has lived in New York since the late sixties, and is now at work on a novel.

MARKS

You'll have to go Mr. Shape, she says, opening the door to his room without knocking. She is dressed in white from head to foot, a white nurse-nun-housekeeper, white face, white hands, eyes of a yellowish-beige to provide a little discreet color. She cannot be touched mentally or physically by reason of the impenetrable whiteness which protects her from the assaults of the richly colored world of browns and greens and grays into which she has stepped.

Oh? he says, wanting to say, knock before you enter, bitch, damn your eyes, but finding himself under some tongue-paralysis that keeps the old wagger frozen in its tracks.

Yes, she says, writing her name in the dust on the top of the chest of drawers, which obtrudes into the room, being too large for the height, width, depth of the attic where it finds itself.

Why? he asks, not really wanting to hear. It has happened before in other lodgings, this bursting in out of the blue, this ordering out. What can she tell him?

It's the marks, she says obligingly, and then pretends to look embarrassed, draws a heart in the dust and labels it Shape. Draws an arrow to stab said Shape to its vitals.

What marks? He is daring her to come out and say which marks in particular he is being accused of.

There's different sorts, she says, shrugging her shoulders. It isn't a question of one kind of mark alone.

Oh. He sees that the trouble is deep-seated, and unlikely to disappear quickly.

I could forgive one kind, she says, I'm not a hard woman. It is the multiplicity of marks that I find intolerable.

I see.

I blame myself in part, she says lightly, not blaming herself for a moment. I have my limitations, haven't I?

Oh. He wonders what they could be, what effect they could have in a confined space.

The extraordinary variety of marks you have left about to show that you have lived for three months in my best back room is too much for me to bear. They're turning up in my dreams, aren't they?

They turn up in mine, he says grinning, so why shouldn't they turn up in yours too? It isn't a question of one's position in life, is it? It isn't education. You're one of nature's ladies, so why not? He grins again stupidly, so that she gets a dazzling view of the plaque-covered beauties. He has mistaken her mood, which is a most unfortunate error for him to make at this stage of the proceedings. Believe you me, and he is still ignorant of his blunder. I know exactly how you feel. He has made another mistake, still more serious than the first. She is on him, moving faster than he could have dreamed.

Oh no. Oh no you don't know how I feel. You think you do, but that's because it's convenient to think you do. You don't really know at all. You're putting on an act, hoping to wriggle out of this one and still inhabit my best back room. I was prepared to give you a second chance, but a second chance is quite out of the question after a remark like that.

What marks then? He is getting a bit aggressive. If all is lost he might as well go down fighting slightly, for that is how it is done.

Soup marks, she says warily, and sniffs.

Where? Where are the soup marks? he demands, counsel for the defence rising to his feet to see if it will help at all. It's all very well for you standing there with your arms folded, looking down your nose, but just you show me where the marks are, the soup marks.

There is one on the carpet, between your feet. Reddish-brown windsor, it shows up dreadfully on the delicate pale green. He jumps, nervous. Has she got him? Is this it? He studies the place in question, giving it his close attention. Said spot or mark is illuminated by a weak and seedy strand of sunshine which has found a way between two warehouses across the street.

Pale green, he sneers. Delicate dirty green is a better description of the exquisite shade in question. That carpet's so dirty, a bit of extra brown windsor isn't going to do anything except improve it, and it just so happens dear lady, that what you are looking at is mulligatawny.

There were soup marks on the sheets last week, and that's not all, not by a long chalk. She is getting her rage properly wound up, and if she can keep it going she will be white in the face and quivering.

Tell me about all, he says, sneering, arms akimbo, copying her stance as best he can — being frightened of her, he hopes to frighten her back by the oldest method in the world, crass imitation.

Sperm, she roars. Sperm on the sheets, sperm on the bedspread, ruining the silvery finish, sperm on the towels, sperm on the carpet. There's even sperm on the walls of this room, which was freshly redecorated not two days before you moved in; not two days, not three months ago.

He sighs. Semen, he says wearily, superior in a tight corner. Semen.

I know what I know, she says, it's all the same to me. Sperm, semen, who cares? The previous tenant had to go. He cut his throat if you must know, and the blood soaked into the plaster, you know how difficult blood is. I can't help it if blood's difficult, now can I?

No! Is it really difficult? he says, daring a sarcasm which he believes to be known only to himself. I had no idea that there was anything difficult about blood at all.

Well, now you know don't you? You know it's difficult, and you know the last tenant had to go. You've got to go because marks are also difficult — and the sooner the better.

Oh. He has no answer to that. He feels saddened by her accusations, her denunciations of him and his. Life in the room appears to be at a full stop, the next paragraph has not appeared over the horizon. It won't come until it's ready, which may be never. She sees she has bludgeoned him into a mental heap, and is sorry to vanquish. After all, she'd only been picking on him, hadn't she, just to see what he'd do?

You'll have to go, that's the beginning and end of it. Don't think I'm going to waste any pity on you either, Mr.

Shape. If you hadn't come here in the first place, you would never have had to leave, never. You've only got yourself to blame. Almost regretfully it seems, she wipes out the heart, leaving only the label to mark its absence: Shape.

GAPS

'They'll be well looked after, all those dear little gaps,' the nurse said, as she shaved Patient 4 from head to foot, leaving odd tufts here and there, random selection as you might say. The nurse whistled while she worked, shaving always cheered her up, she found the human body more creative than mowing the lawn, trimming the hedge. The ins and outs tested her artistic skill, the steadiness of her hand. The tune she whistled was entitled 'Nearer my God to Thee'.

'When Mr Rod has done his scissors and paste feel, dressed like a banker, not a speck on his black jacket, his immaculate black soul, you won't even know they're gone. You'll feel ever so much better. Mr Rod's our head stylist in the gap department, surgically speaking. Do you know that he wrote the definition of scalpel himself? Of course that's a very grand word, speaks volumes doesn't it? You won't have to worry about a word like that, a bit beyond your range really, isn't it? The implications dear, that's what I mean. Don't be offended, we can't all be stars. Just you lie back and leave the fancy footwork to Mr Rod.' The nurse had stars in her yellow eyes, but they did not show up too well.

'All the same, just think of the honour. He is an artist of the cut and thrust, and ever so particular is Mr Rod. His speedy assaults on female patients are a byword in the trade. That chart on his wall, the one with the little colored flags, you must have seen it. Yes, that is a record for posterity that is. I've heard him on the intercom, he's ever so firm, puts his black-shod foot down, doesn't he? Why do you know Patient 4 that he has developed a new and wonderfully exciting technique whereby he operates upon the psyche with steely polished fingernails caked with a rim of specially mixed mourning prepared in his very own laboratory from the finest blends of high quality filth? Do you know that he'll persuade you with one sorry glance that you're suffering from mastitis, vaginal infections, clitoral infections, mental infections, spleen infections, potential infections, Patient 4, of every sort you ever imagined? If you thought you knew the ins and outs of your hypochondrias, take a back seat Patient 4 I'm warning you. And all this persuasiveness after only five minutes conversation, applied to patient once a year over a five-year period. Now that's efficiency that is, he has quite a way with words. That is the result of time and motion studies, that is the result of nameless pressures applied with wonderful subtlety.'

The nurse was loyal, ever so loyal

'It was for your own good Patient 4,' said Mr Rod, greasy black hair smoothed down, parting straight, ears clean, smirking as he tugged at his striped trousers and sat himself down by her bedside. He always liked to flatter the private patients, for who knows when they might decide to come back for another go. However, on this occasion he was practising flattery upon a state-financed cow, to see if it had the same effect — part of a research project he was indulging himself in at the expense of others. Who knows she might come back for another go inspired by the winged diagnoses flying out of his thin mouth, plirp-plirp, plirp-plirp. The body is full of errors, rich in them indeed, all grist to the mill.

Together Mr Rod and Patient 4 watched the vital signs of her tiny collection of remaining gaps dancing clumsily upon the screen: amateur night without the booing. He smiled at her unpleasantly while her heavily-bandaged dictionary slowly leaked a puddle of blood and pus through its binding, lest she forget do you see, lest she forget. Once the gap has been cut away and the place neatly sewn up, it is hard to remember exactly what was where, hence the dictionary, brought in as a consultant with its thumb index ever at the ready.

DEATH CAR

For Torquay and all after

— I am driving the death car, a pre-war model, softly spoken engine. It bears its intricacies lightly in its elegant body running on two wheels in the front, one at the back. The death car transports those who live in the mind's eye, whether the living or the dead, present or absent. You are active in as many different dimensions as there are memories of you, and you have no choice in the matter, either in this life or the next. Perhaps you are happy in one person's memory, while in another's you are seen in three-quarter profile, your attitude ambiguous; to a third your existence is bitter pain bleeding away at the edges of anger. To a lover you are one to hold, to an old friend one who cooks chicken livers, to a sister, one who is immersed in some private and unexplained act of vengeance upon the world. Let only one person in the world hear at third hand that you fish, then you will fish. Alive or dead, it doesn't matter in the least, down to the river you will go to catch fish.

— All my driving has been done at the wheel of the death car, no license, no insurance, a vehicle alone upon the road, passing the ghosts of cars driving through another world. I drive and am driven, while my passengers bring their monologues together that they may give birth to whole conversations, the descendants of the warm sea monologues of amoebas considering whether they should, or whether they should not — split; and coming to the inevitable moment and splitting to create two-part discussions upon the subject of division, its pain and its necessity, which in time spread across the world putting down roots of memory to sustain themselves — prohibition, trouble and delay, roots which hold them firmly in the soil.

— What's the name of this place? I ask, eyes on the blacktop road, thinking to catch my passengers with nothing to say, for the road shows no sign of passing through any place. It vanishes into the distance between high winter hedges, a faint scratch of a crossroads a mile or so away.

— Abscess, my passengers shout. We'll show you on the map, driver, we have a map which shows it clearly.

— Abscess. It's always Abscess. They have yet to show me the map. As we pass, I glance quickly through a gap in the hedge and see that Abscess on this occasion is steep gray hills running down to a gray sea. Abandoned villages are dug into hollows and folds in a land empty of people, desolate with the coarse, dry grass that grows after sheep have eaten the land to the bone, and moved on.

— Those villages were inhabited by the pre-sheep people, one of my passengers says, cheerful for some reason of her own. Your ancestors, driver, were driven out of their homes to make room for a woolly cash crop which destroyed the land. I can hear a smile in my passenger's voice as she speaks again. Now even the sheep have gone, she says, and laughs to herself, satisfied with the turn of events.

— The roofs have caved in, I say.

— They're always the first to go, she says, sure of the order of business.

— You should have told me it was a death car, I say, slowing to look four ways at the crossroads, and deciding to go straight on. I thought. I was sure. An outing, that's what I thought. An outing. We would go out, that was the understanding, for a drive, for a bit of a drive, then home for tea. My passengers exchange glances around me, ducking to avoid the rearview mirror in case they should reveal something they wish to keep private from me.

— To fail as a lookout is to be banished for a lifetime, for an eternity, from the company of those who rely upon your perception, one says, non-committal, staring at a crow perched on a gate.

— Home! You're trying to get away with something driver. We never said that. Quickly now, quickly, we'll be late for the ceremonies, quickly now. Keep an eye on the road driver, report upon the fine nuances of the view, lookout, for you are the lookout. That's all a driver of the death car ever is, a lookout, one who sees and then speaks upon the subject that others may hear and know. You are an interpreter, who must describe for the rest of us an approaching army stumbling through vegetable gardens, field mice, a hawk, an owl, a low-sailing cloud, a rainstorm in the distance, sunshine behind it; a mighty wicker god, stuffed with weeping men watching the flaming torch carried at a run from out of the silent crowd of spectators, and across the empty stretch of ground below the fort. Events. In order to exist, the interpreter must describe what she sees, must look carefully into the eyes of those who weep and as carefully into the eyes of those who watch. Catch the look on the torch bearer's face, understand how it will be with the god after the feeding, and tell us about these things, so that we will be sure of what it was that took place. If she fails to do so, she will vanish. One of them leans over and laughs harshly in my ear.

— You can drive faster than that, step on the gas, driver. Change into that better gear, the private one that doesn't appear on the stick shift diagram. The subtle, soft gear which made itself known to you as though by chance and slipped us into that dimension, remember the one? It was only the other day.

— That's how they are. That's how they always are. The death car is running nicely.

IV
HINGES

A play in three acts

Sorel Etrog

Photograph by Michel Nguyen

Sorel Etrog was born in 1933 in Jassy, Roumania and began his formal art training in 1945. He emigrated to Israel and held his first one-man show in Tel Aviv in 1958. Subsequently he received a scholarship to Brooklyn Museum Art Inst. In 1961 he set up his studio in Toronto and settled there permanently in 1963. He was one of three artists representing Canada at the Venice Biennale in 1966. Since then he has become one of the best known contemporary artists working mostly in sculpture, but also in other forms and in the theatre for which he writes, directs and designs. He met Samuel Beckett in Paris in the late 1960's and illustrated *Imagination Dead Imagine* in a limited numbered edition.

Notes by Marshall McLuhan

Hinges is a structuralist play in which Etrog dispenses with the diatronique in favour of the synchronique. People as iconic, include all possible levels of meaning and experience, yet are immediately physical presences. They are trapped in a search for private identity and meaning which seems to be inaccessible.

In the first Act, Booing with the Public, *we go outside for privacy. In the second Act,* The Wallpaper, *we go inside and encounter a shattered privacy. In the third Act,* The Tomato Bush, *there is no inside or outside — the fourth world of electric space takes over. The computerized American gets a funeral plot with his pension and his social security kit. Housing is out of the question. It's cheaper now to die or to accept early retirement.*

ACT I – Booing With The Public

In the first Act we see man, the servo-mechanism, the docile robot of his own bodily extensions, the well-adjusted man who has lost all private identity. He is a married man with a child, an honest consumer, an ordinary man who puts on his trousers one leg at a time. With the loss of identity through social adjustment, he has lost the power of communicating. He is a gadget lover, like Babbitt in the novel of Sinclair Lewis. He lives in *The Waste Land* of T.S. Eliot. After this nuclear family has poured itself into their three monitors, the mass man goes out into the crowd in his sarcophagus to achieve privacy. As he closes the lid of the coffin, there is the roar of a football crowd heard from within, during the pause for station identification.

The *figure*, enveloped in the mystical cycle of value, price, profit and rent, is seen in the *ground* of the apartment which is an extension of the super highway world. He steps from one 'death' to another. In his sarcophagus he is free to seek privacy and identity. At home he has no privacy or identity.

ACT II – The Wall Paper

The Wall Paper is concerned with the Americanization of Europe: *Le Défi Américain*. The fourth world, the electric world, as it envelops Europe, transforms the pattern of the patriarchal family and ends the reign of privacy at home. (cf. *The Discrete Charm of the Bourgeoisie* by Bunuel.) Whereas the norm of European privacy had been to go inside to be

alone, this is no longer possible with the electric media —
telephone, radio, TV — invading the home in all the
sensory modes. Privacy now shifts to the outer world for the
European as for the American, but the conflict between the
old norm and the new form is still intense.

The Wall Paper is, in a way, the unfolding of the vertical
rings of a tree, and presents the home as a sanctuary for
privacy — roll playing and role playing. The wifely routine
has already confirmed that the husband is 'dead', a
prisoner of her trivial 'sock' rituals. In the First Act he had
been a prisoner or servo-mechanism of the private
extensions of his own body. In the Second Act he is the
prisoner of the conventional group social routines which
stress private life. He pursues identity by adopting the most
extreme roles, oscillating between the role of prisoner and
judge, the judge being the rebel ghost image of old
patriarchal ascendancy. The home is transformed into a
courtroom of altercation and dispute, managed by police
whistles. The judge wears TV and puts on his robes as his
public. The family becomes the jury, the extended family,
lined up against the individual. The woman becomes
matriarchal head of the extended family, and the
patriarchal 'head' becomes a prisoner of the domestic game
rituals, a little boy with his bottle and his teddy bear. Later
in the play the new matriarch decides to put her head in the
trivial noose together with her husband in order that both
can hang together rather than hang separately. In Act Two
there arises a new conflict in the world of privacy in-doors.
By leaving his new commune home (peopled by the electric
media) he resumes his quest for private identity and, by
joining the army, falls into another collective trap.

'Order in the court! The accused will now make a
bogus statement.'

Ulysses (p. 587)

ACT III – The Tomato Bush

— all wire and fire
— the burning bush

In the Third Act man is suffoclosed — a dropout in a world where everything relates to everything, yet all is out of touch, i.e., a classic paranoid situation such as is present in Levi-Strauss' *The Savage Mind*. 'Is you feeling like you is lost in the bush, boy?' (*Finnegans Wake* — Joyce). The savage is aware that everything affects everything in his acoustic world, and this is itself a paranoid state. It is the archetype of Eliot's *Crocodile Isle*. The approach of the 'investigator', the pet dog, threatens his *querencia*, his internal space.

O keep the Dog far hence that's friend to man

T.S. Eliot

In a world where there is no inside or outside, the only *out* is an inner trip. On the wired planet, the bugged earth, man's privacy is found only by the inner trip. Craving contact, he is electrocuted by a newscast. Civilization, with its private individuals, is transformed into the tribal horde of the fourth world, the global village.

Marshall McLuhan
1975

ACT I

BOOING WITH THE PUBLIC

(Prisoner of Habit)

Characters

A man in his late 30's
A woman, his wife, 30
A little boy, his son, 8 years old.

Scene i

Setting: a small room furnished with a bed, and kitchenette with a toaster, an electric coffee pot in left corner, a little dining table with a place setting for one person. There are two or three framed reproductions on the wall, a sink with towels, an old television set, a bird cage (but no bird), a mirror, and a rocking chair opposite the television. There is an entrance door stage right and a window next to the door.

The stage is dark. We hear a key turning in the lock. The man enters and turns on the light. The room is dimly lit. He throws his briefcase, coat and hat on the chair, takes off his clothes and puts on his pyjamas, gets washed and brushes his teeth. He turns on the bedside light, shuts off the main light, gets into bed, turns off the lamp and goes to sleep. The stage is pitch dark. We hear a slight snoring. After ten to fifteen seconds of snoring, an alarm suddenly rings, the sound greatly amplified. The man jumps out of bed, pulls the curtain aside, washes himself quickly at the sink, dresses himself rapidly, puts on the electric coffee pot, all the while running from one activity to the other. He puts a piece of bread in the toaster while doing up his pants. The coffee pot whistles loudly just as he has his coat on and briefcase in hand. Suddenly realizing that he doesn't have time for breakfast, he grabs the coffee pot, closes the kitchenette curtains and runs out the door. (The coffee pot whistle is heard after he leaves). The stage becomes pitch black. A few seconds later, we hear the key turning in the door. The man enters the room. The room is dimly lit. He looks for the chair. He cannot find it. He throws his hat, coat and briefcase on the bed. He loosens his tie and turns on the television. The back of the television set faces the audience, and so the screen lights his face. We hear the sound of changing channels, and we see him in the rocking chair facing the television. Next to him is a little bag from which he takes a pop can and sandwich. He rocks in the chair, chewing the sandwich and drinking from the can. From the television we hear the noise of a football game. He jumps up with excitement and sits down again, finishes the sandwich and throws the bag behind him, finishes the can of pop and throws the can behind him, finishes another can of pop and throws the can behind him, finishes yet another can of pop and throws it behind him. The light dims slowly. We hear him snoring as the television goes on. Suddenly we hear the alarm clock ringing again. He gets up and opens the curtains. Full morning light pours in. The television is still on. We notice that the kitchen table has become covered with a mountain of empty pop cans. On the floor is a pile of sandwich bags and all kinds of boxes and more empty pop cans. As he wades through this rubble he has a hard time finding his briefcase and coat, etc. He leaves the room still half asleep, tie loose, clothes rumpled. He kicks one of the empty cans like a football as he leaves the room. The television is still on. The stage is darkened. He returns a moment later and, neatly clothed and a fresh can in his hand turns on the lights. He goes to the table, smashes the pop cans on the floor (amplified smash). He plugs the coffee pot in, sits in the rocking chair in front of the television, changing rapidly from channel to channel to channel and then in disgust, throws the T.V. up in the air, and it lands on the bed. Next, he tumbles over the rocking chair, crawls to the table with difficulty, then overturns the table as well. After this destruction, during which he remains fully dressed, he attempts to get up and collapses on the floor—a hard landing. The T.V. continues to play on the bed as the curtain falls. On the curtain a football game is projected, and loud noises from the football fans are heard for about 45 seconds. The noise and the projection stop abruptly leaving the curtain dark.

Scene ii

The curtain goes up, and we hear the key again turning in the lock. The man enters the room and turns on the lights. The room is arranged neatly. There is now a woman in a second rocking chair next to the man's. She too has her own television set facing her with its back to the audience. We hear dialogue from it. Next to each television set there is a little table, and on each table a pop can with a straw. The man turns on his T.V., bends to kiss the woman on the cheek as she continues to watch her television. He plunges into his rocking chair full of excitement and watches his television. She rises, goes to get his slippers, bends and kisses him on the cheek, meanwhile keeping her head turned towards her T.V. She returns to her chair. The man sips his pop through the straw. We hear from his T.V. another football game. On her T.V. we continue to hear a romantic dialogue. Each of them turns their sound up louder and louder as the light dims. When it is pitch black the T.V. sounds die as well.

We hear the couple snoring, one at a time and then together. Suddenly two alarm clocks ring one after the other with two different pitches. As morning light pours in from the window we hear a long coffee pot whistle. There are now three television sets running simultaneously and an eight year-old boy in a small rocking chair sits in front of the smallest T.V. from which is heard a Walt Disney cartoon. He is seated between the two larger chairs and rocking. The three rock, and watch, chew and sip from pop cans, their eyes fixed on their sets. They sit so that they all watch individually, never looking at one another. The stage becomes black amidst all this infernal noise.

Scene iii

A cemetery with a few tombstones is seen in the background. In the centre is a coffin with the lid open. Around it, a little procession takes place. The man is carrying a television. The woman behind him carries an alarm clock and a steaming coffee pot. Behind her, the small boy carries some pop cans and a large sandwich bag. With excitement the man puts the television in the coffin, takes off his coat, throws it and his hat inside and gets into the coffin. The woman puts the coffee pot and the alarm clock in the coffin. We hear the amplified ticking of the clock becoming louder and louder. The man kisses his wife on both cheeks. The little boy comes to his father, gives him the pop can and the bag with a sandwich. The man kisses the boy on both cheeks. The boy and the woman step back, still facing the coffin. They are in the dark now, with the light only on the man in the coffin. The man, unaware of them, opens the sandwich bag, takes a big bite, chews, sips from the pop straw, winds up the alarm clock, turns on the television to another football game. The coffee pot is whistling. He closes the lid of the coffin above him as the noise of excited football fans is heard from within. The light dims to black very slowly. The noise continues and stops abruptly when the stage is black.

ACT II

THE WALLPAPER

(A Game)

Mr. Y, a man in his mid 30's
a prisoner
a judge
a military man (all played by Mr. Y)
Mrs. Y, a woman in her early 30's
Two children, aged 8 and 10

Mourners:
- Two middle-aged men
- Two men in their early 20's
- Two middle-aged woman
- Two children,

Jurors:
- Two middle-aged men
- Two middle-aged women
- Two children

Assistants, make-up man, camera man, lights man; all played by the men in their early 20's.

Note:
The Shiva, is the Jewish mourning ritual, which lasts seven days and it is compulsory for the mourners to wear black socks.

Scene i

BEDROOM (Down-stage)

The lights come up slowly as the curtain rises until they reveal the feet and the lower legs of four men, three women and two children (all their feet are in black socks) walking around in a circle slowly as if in a funeral procession. As the light is raised, we see that the four men are carrying a coffin on their shoulders. All the faces are veiled from the nose down with a thin, black veil. The men are dressed in black business suits, and black shirts. (All blacks are matte except for the black ties which are shiny.) The women are dressed in black dresses with black bras (of shiny material) on top of the dresses. The two children are wearing black sports suits, with shiny belts and carrying long black candles. They circle a bed covered with an ornate lace bedspread. Dim lights. We see the movement under the covers of a couple making love. We hear the amplified sound of the bedsprings creaking and giggles and groans while the procession continues around the bed. They all stop at once – the procession and the lovemaking. After ten seconds Mrs. Y descends from the bed. She is wearing a black nightgown. She puts on a black veil to cover her face. Then she remains motionless in front of the bed. The pallbearers place the coffin to her left. The foot of the coffin is facing the audience, the head slightly raised about 8″ so that the audience can have a perspective view of the coffin. On the lid of the coffin a small barred window can be seen. The two children place themselves on either side of the coffin and light their candles. The pallbearers open the coffin. They remove from inside a small black laundry basket which they place directly in front of Mrs. Y. Then they remove Mr. Y from the bed and place him in the coffin. A faint funeral march is heard as they start to circle Mrs. Y, the coffin and the bed. As they circle for the second time, each member of the procession stops in front of Mrs. Y, bows to her discreetly, and, removing their socks, they place them in the laundry basket and continue to circle. As they circle further, the funeral march becomes louder. A crack in the record established a limping rhythm. The procession begins to limp as well. They circle one more time and stop. Mrs. Y kneels in front of the coffin as in prayer. The children and mourners leave the stage. Mrs. Y then mounts the coffin as if on a horse with her back to the audience, so that her crotch covers the window. The light dims as two small spots light Mrs. Y's naked buttocks, for a few seconds. A long whistle of a coffee pot is heard as the lights gradually fade to black.

Scene ii

THE PRISON (Stage right)

Stage black. Loud storm sounds are accompanied by a few flashes of lightening. The sound of heavy rain diminishes to raindrops. Then the metal clanking noise of a prison door opening. Dim light. A man is pushed in and falls to the floor. The door clashes shut. The man gets up with difficulty, goes to the prison door and shakes it in despair. A woman's sharp giggle is heard as he continues to shake the door. We hear a boxing gong sound and an arena crowd cheer as he shakes the door more and more intensely. The woman's giggles become more hysterical. Another gong rings. The man callapses on the floor (hard landing). The crowd noisily counts down, ONE (giggle) TWO (giggle) THREE (giggle). Each count comes from a different part of the stage. Not knowing from where the sound is coming, he turns his head and body from side to side.

Light dims to black as the countdown fades.

In dim light the prisoner gets up. Two assistants appear who dress him as a judge in a long robe and long curly white, wig. He wears black socks and through the wig we see a piece of the prisoner's cap.

Scene iii
COURTROOM (Stage left)
Medium light. A small courtroom with a bare window at the back wall. To the right of the window three feet away, at an angle facing the audience, is the judge's bench and the jury's bench. The jury is made up of three men and two women and two children. They have veils over their eyes and noses, and whistles in their mouths. They are wearing black robes and white wigs. The judge walks in majestically. The jury stands up. The judge goes to his bench and sits down. He too has a whistle in his mouth which he blows, signalling with his hand for the jury to sit down. They all land at once on their seats noisily like schoolchildren. The judge and jury struggle to put on enormous earphones with attached mouthpieces. They mount them with some difficulty on top of their wigs. The two children have only one pair of earphones between them. They stretch the earphones around their heads, thus enabling each child to have one ear covered by an earphone. In front of every juror is an old typewriter, and a pad of paper. On the judge's desk is an enormous typewriter and a huge wooden hammer. Two make-up men enter. They fix the judge's prison cap, the wig and the hair which, at this point, shows even more because of the earphones. All this as the judge is looking at himself in the mirror. The mirror is placed on the typewriter so the judge can see his own contented expression. All the jury are fixing themselves up as well with little mirrors leaning against the small typewriters in front of them. One of the make-up men is taking floodlights out of a suitcase. The lights are directed on the judge. The other man is putting an empty T.V. set over the judge's head so the judge's head is seen through the hole for the screen. There is a broad smile on his face. The first man puts a large movie camera on his shoulder. He is filming the judge as the judge is trying out a few different shaped whistles. He settles for one which remains in his mouth. Then he stands up, tries to lift the

hammer, can't, tumbles back into his chair, and gets up again. The juryman next to him helps him to lift the hammer, and they lift it together above their heads, but the hammer slips out of their hands and drops noisily behind the judge's chair. The judge, very annoyed, with a brusque movement, blows the whistle, spits, blows it again and finally it makes a sound like a fart. The judge angrily pulls the T.V. set from his head, and throws it in the air. The camera man stands up and motions hysterically for them to leave. Then he chases them offstage as they hurriedly drag their equipment behind as the light in the courtroom dims to black for a few seconds. In the dark we hear a humming of a lullaby coming from offstage. As the humming becomes louder, a followspot lights Mrs. Y as she enters the courtroom pushing and rocking a huge pram which is the coffin on wheels. She stops at the centre of the courtroom. She then mounts the coffin as a coffee pot whistle is heard. She continues to hum the lullaby. After a few seconds she gets off the coffin. As she steps down, we see the judge's head rising slowly through the window of the lid of the coffin. A bewildered sound comes from the jury now in the dark. Mrs. Y stretches her hands towards the judge's head, removes his wig which reveals his prisoner's cap. The jury giggles. She places the judge's wig on her head. More giggles. She grabs his whistle and tries to throw it away, but it is attached to the judge with a rubber band and snaps back into his face. The jury is roaring with laughter. She clasps his cheeks with both hands and kisses him at length on the mouth as we hear the cheering crowd of a sports arena. Suddenly, the judge, having had enough of that, pulls away from Mrs. Y, jumps out of the coffin as the light rises in the courtroom. He then takes the wig from Mrs. Y's head and puts it back on his head. He closes the coffin lid and places his whistle back into his mouth. The jury is in an uproar. Blowing his whistle, he summons the courtroom to order. Mrs. Y is motionless. The judge walks around her and like a detective 'investigates' her and the pram while Mrs. Y continues to hum the lullaby. Suddenly, he stops in front of her with one foot remaining in the air. (Mrs. Y stops humming.) With his left hand he forces the whistle from his mouth making the sound of a cork coming out from a bottle. He looks at his whistle, is not satisfied and tries another one. He hides it behind his back and immediately puts it back in

Hinges

his mouth, a movement which looks like mouth to ass– ass to mouth, whistling each time as the whistle comes to his mouth. Once in a while, he moves his hands threateningly, as if accusing Mrs. Y. All this while he is still on one foot. The jury is cheering him and banging on their desks. The judge looks back to the jury. Content, with a broad smile on his face, he stamps his foot down with a loud bang, landing on his other foot. Annoyed and limping, he goes back to his bench. He looks at the jury with authority, his arm outstretched, pointing with index finger at Mrs. Y as if aiming a gun. He holds this position for a few seconds, turns his head towards the jury for approval. Then all nod their heads. We hear a loud gun shot. Mrs. Y collapses next to the coffin. There is great agitation among the members of the jury. The camera man and assistant reappear and with great speed set up floodlights directed on Mrs. Y and the judge and put TV sets on their heads. The camera man starts shooting and the other takes photographs. The members of the jury step down from their bench, mumbling and grumbling through their whistles to one another. The judge orders the camera man and photographer to leave. They pick up their cameras and their floodlights and run. The stage is a bit darker now that all the floodlights have gone. One of the jurors tumbles over Mrs. Y. He is picked up by another, stands up, and takes a look at Mrs. Y's corpse which makes him jump with fear. He removes the lid of the coffin, and, reluctantly, puts his hand inside. There is a broad smile on his face as he takes out pop cans and passes them around to the judge and the jury. They all remove their whistles, open the pop cans all at once and drink to the health of the judge. He goes back to the coffin and this time takes out the basket full of black socks. He puts the basket on the judge's desk. The judge picks up one of the socks from the basket, holds it high above his head, studies the sock inside-out, brings it to his nose and smells it at length. He passes the sock to the jurors, who each begin to study and smell the sock in the same manner. The judge inserts a large paper into his huge typewriter and types a few letters, puts his whistle back in his mouth, picks up another sock which he passes to the jury until each member has a sock in his hand. They all begin to type simultaneously and a wild *concertina* of amplified typewriter sounds is heard. The stage goes black as the sound stops.

Scene iv

THE PRISON

The same lullaby is heard as the stage is lit softly. The prisoner is on the floor wearing an enormous diaper. His prisoner's cap is large enough to cover part of his face. He is trying to remove the one sock he is wearing. Through the window-bars we see the bare breasts of a woman pushing themselves through the bars. The prisoner is distracted from removing his sock, and with outstretched arms walks toward the window bars we see a hand turning a coloured rattle. backwards noisily with a cry, picks up a pop bottle with a nipple, starts sucking and laughing like a baby. He is distracted by two balloons bouncing in and starts playing with them as the breasts at the window disappear. Through bars of the window we see a hand turning a coloured rattle. He looks in the direction of the rattle, then ignores it. He gets back to playing with his foot, and takes off the sock, all this to the sound of the rattle. He brings it to his nose, sniffs it, spits on it, and then throws the sock away. The stage dims to black. (The amplified rattle sound continues through the change of scenes).

Scene v

COURTROOM

The judge is lost in his thoughts as he plays with his rattle. The coffin is no longer present in the courtroom. Soft light reveals the judge and the jury in the arrangement of Rembrandt's 'Anatomy Lesson'. On the jury bench, strongly lit, Mrs. Y lies dead. She is veiled and dressed in a transparent black nightgown through which her naked body can be seen. The jury stands around Mrs. Y motionless as the judge continues to play with the rattle. Then one juror picks up one sock at a time from the basket and passes it beneath the nose of the dead woman. As the fourth sock is passed beneath her nose, she jumps up. The judge and the jury are startled by this sudden revival. She snatches the sock from the hand of the juror, runs towards the judge, kisses him quickly on the mouth and jumps through the barred window. The stage becomes black. We hear the sound of glass smashing through to the next scene.

Scene vi

PRISON CELL AND COURTROOM (seen simultaneously)

PRISON CELL	COURTROOM
The sound of the smashed glass stops as bright light shows the prisoner on the floor collecting large pieces of stained glass. He plays noisily with them. The bottle which he was previously sucking is now broken and he places it between his legs like a penis. He tears off a piece of cloth from his diaper, bandages the broken bottle, as the funeral march is heard again louder and louder, then suddenly dies.	The jury flocks around the window from which Mrs Y jumped. We see them talking two by two with their whistles in their mouths, looking out the window, changing whistles with one another in agitation, and carrying on a grumbling conversation. One of the jurors is imitating the judge in jest. They all giggle through their whistles. One of the jury suggests knotting two socks together. Then they knot all the socks into a long rope and line up like soldiers.

Stage darkens as both scenes end simultaneously.

Scene vii

THE COURTROOM

The judge is alone in the courtroom, seemingly lost in meditation. Both thumbs are in his mouth and his eight fingers are covering his eyes. We hear the tramping of the feet of the jury offstage coming closer and closer. The judge takes his thumbs out of his mouth, looks at them, hides them behind his back, quickly picks up two whistles from the desk and puts them in his mouth, and blows them loudly. The jurors then march in one by one holding the rope with both hands above their heads. They circle the judge and then line up. The judge steps down from his desk, checks the end of the rope for strength (facing the window), walks to the window with the end of the rope and pulls it slowly from their hands. He makes a lasso-loop from the end of the rope and twists it around his hand like a cowboy, throws it through the window and almost falls with it. (As he is bent over the window, we notice the judge's buttocks exposed under his robes; two pin spots should focus on the buttocks). As this happens, one of the jurors catches him, pulls him back from falling over, covers his buttocks with his robes, and all the jurors look at one another giggling through their whistles with embarrassment. Infuriated, the judge changes whistles (different sounds for each) rapidly making irritated noises, aiming his index finger at the whole group of the jury. They all have their hands above their heads. His index finger goes down. They lower their hands. As they line up again, he gives them the end of the lasso, gives them a long whistle which sounds like a fart, and begins sniffing back strongly, clearing his throat (dry saliva sound) and keeping time by a bang of the foot, as the jury men begin pulling the rope as though they were bringing up a heavy body. The judge's foot continues to bang. A slave's song is heard in the background. The courtroom grows dark as the only light is coming from the window.

Scene viii

PRISON

In the middle of the cell the prisoner stands on the bed. The bed is covered with an ornate lace bedspread. The floor is covered by balloons like colourful clouds. The rope made of socks hangs from the ceiling above the bed. The prisoner stands on the bed with his head through the hanging loop and he looks upward towards the ceiling, holding his thumbs in his mouth and the bandaged bottle between his legs. On the right side of the bed a black-veiled mourner with a black heard holds a black book in one hand and the rattle in the other. The mourner looks at the prisoner for a long time, then gives him the rattle. The prisoner takes his thumbs from his mouth as he receives the rattle. The mourner kneels, facing the audience. He is directly below the prisoner on the floor between the balloons. He opens his black book, and starts rocking backwards and forwards, looking up towards heaven and giving the impression of praying, while the prisoner spins the rattle above his head. The rattling becomes louder and louder as the mourner continues to pray. Suddenly the bearded mourner puts down the book and undresses to the waist revealing two exposed breasts. It is Mrs. Y. She then gets up on the bed next to the prisoner, gently places her head on his shoulder for a few seconds and then slowly expands the loop around the prisoner's head wide enough for both heads to fit. She inserts her own head with that of the prisoner, and produces a pop can with a straw. They each take a sip, and she holds the prisoner's hand which holds the rattle so that they now both spin it together. As the stage dims to black, the rattling sound is substituted by a long male-female giggle which then turns into a long erotic laugh.

Scene ix

COURTYARD OF A SUBURBAN HOUSE
(Down-stage)

The stage is fully lit with a blue sky background showing a few trees. To the right we see the pink wall of a house. A clothes-line is stretched from one of the trees towards the house. In the background we hear light music from a radio. On the window-ledge there are some flower pots. Mrs. Y, humming the tune of the radio, carries a basket of socks (very colourful ones of primary colours). While humming she hangs the socks on the line. Mr. Y walks in with dignity. He is in a military uniform and carries a knapsack on his back, a rifle on his shoulder, and a small radio from which the music is heard. He looks up at the blue sky. We hear some birds singing. He rests his rifle and radio on the ground close to Mrs. Y. As he puts them down the birdsong stops. He switches off the radio. Mrs. Y stops pegging the socks. At the window of the house, the two children appear with whistles in their mouths, playing with one another, sucking their whistles, making grumbling noises and giggling as Mrs. Y clasps Mr. Y's cheeks with her hands and kisses him at length. A long strident whistle from a coffee pot is heard as the curtain falls.

ACT III

THE TOMATO BUSH

(Deadend)

Characters

A Soldier in his middle 20's
A Young Boy aged 10
A Woman in her early 30's (the boy's mother)
A Man in his early 40's (the boy's father)
A Woman in her late 60's (the boy's grandmother)
A Man in his 70's, with a beard (the boy's grandfather).

Scene i

The stage is filled with summer light. We hear birds singing; the countryside has large tomato bushes supported on wooden stakes, and each bush has three or four large ripe red tomatoes. We also hear a cow's moos and other farmyard noises and then suddenly the shrieking sound of a low passing jet and simultaneously the stage darkens to black. Night sounds: frogs croaking, etc. We hear the hard landing of a body and groans and heavy breathing of a man. He turns on a flashlight, and we see he is a soldier with a parachute still attached to him and spread out over the stage. He turns off the flashlight. The light is very dim. We can just see him getting out of the parachute harness, still groaning and in pain. He folds the parachute neatly while sitting on the floor and continues to groan. He takes off his knapsack and opens it. While all this goes on, he is turning the flashlight on and off at intervals. We see him opening the knapsack and taking out a canteen. He takes a long sip. We hear a sigh of relief after the drink. He takes out a radio, puts on earphones and listens, but there is no sound. He impatiently taps on the radio which is evidently dead. He is whispering, 'Hello, hello, hello ... ' so as not to be overheard. He tears his pantleg open — groaning again — and takes out a bandage from his knapsack. The flashlight still goes on and off. In the background we hear the sound of shelling, and flashes of light, like lightning, appear on the horizon. He bandages his foot. He tries to get up, collapses with a loud crashing sound. He searches the space around him with the flashlight, makes a little bed from the parachute and lies down on it. He puts the earphones on again to find out if there is any sound. He whispers, 'HELLO! HELLO! HELLO! ... ' The whisper turns into a scream. Louder and louder he screams HELLO! as the shelling sound increases. Then lights and the sounds of the shelling stop abruptly, and we hear him snoring faintly. Suddenly, a spotlight shines on a little boy standing behind the sleeping soldier. He is flying a kite just over his head, and as he is circling the sleeping soldier, the stage light increases slightly; a woman is running after the boy to catch him. Then a man appears, running after the woman, and then an elderly woman runs after him. A bearded elderly man runs after the elderly woman. They run faster and faster circling the soldier. The boy has a slight lead on them, all the while flying his kite. Suddenly we hear the amplified firing of an automatic rifle, and they all collapse except for the little boy. The bodies are pulled offstage as the little boy continues to run with his kite. He circles the soldier once more and then runs off-stage as the light dims again. The soldier rubs his eyes as he wakes from his nightmare. He gets on his knees and turns around quickly, searching for the people. He turns on the flashlight and sees there is nobody around him. He turns it off. He turns it on again to check the time. He turns it off. He rubs his eyes again, then takes out a handkerchief and forcefully blows his nose. He goes back to sleep. He has hardly lain down when the stage is filled with daylight. (The timing should be such that as he lays down his head to sleep, the daylight emerges and he immediately rises). We see the same landscape as at the beginning of the scene with the addition of a few signs which are three to four feet apart and surrounding him. The signs read, DANGER — MINE FIELDS! He rubs his eyes again on account of the daylight. We hear a rooster crow, the birds singing, and other animal sounds. He takes a sip from his canteen and shakes it to see how much is still left in it, unaware of the mine field that he is in. Finally, he tries to get up. He makes a crutch from his gun and starts walking around his parachute bed. He stops in horror and notices with a reaction of panic that he is in the midst of a mine field. He turns a few times quickly, searching to see if there is any escape. As he turns he bangs the floor with his gun crutch in anger. He beats his forehead as if he cannot believe that all this is real. He collapses on the ground in desperation, first on his knees and then face down. He remains in this position for a few seconds. Then slowly he starts crawling around with great care and fear, checking the ground around him with his palm, leaving as a safety mark a standing bullet. He continues to search and mark the safe places until the bullets form a circle which also encloses one of the tomato bushes and his parachute bed. Secure at last, he gives a sigh of relief and surveys his little island. Exhausted, he sits down, wipes the sweat from his forehead, his head turning and searching the horizon all the time. Suddenly we hear dogs barking, and he jumps to his feet. The sudden intrusion alarms him. The barking of the dogs gets closer. He picks up his automatic rifle, removes some of the bullets from the ground, replaces the markers with cigarettes. He loads his rifle. The barking of the dogs is even louder and closer. He aims his rifle at the audience and swings around as though following the running dogs. Then BANG! BANG! BANG! He fires towards the side of the stage. The automatic rifle fire is identical to the sound of the shooting of the poeple we heard earlier. With the final shot the stage goes black. The dying cries of the dogs are heard in the dark a few seconds longer, then the sound fades slowly.

The stage is dimly lit. The soldier is sleeping on his parachute bed. The little boy enters bouncing a huge colourful beach ball. He throws it to the soldier. The soldier gets up with excitement and without limping. They run and pass the ball to one another. The soldier throws it to the DANGER sign; it bounces back. They giggle and make the joyful sounds of children playing. Suddenly the boy disappears with the ball. The stage is brightly lit. The soldier is limping again. He picks up his crutch and looks for the boy. He suddenly realizes that he is outside the safety of his island. Horrified, he plunges back into it. He rests, catching his breath for a few seconds. Then he crawls to his radio, puts on his earphones, taps his radio and screams, 'HELLO! HELLO! HELLO!' He turns it off greatly discouraged and pushes it aside. He pulls out his canteen to take a sip but realizes that it's empty. He throws the canteen on his bed in disgust. He looks around him and suddenly has an idea: there is an expression of hope on his face. His eyes are fixed on a tomato bush. He picks up his crutch and limps towards the bush. He pulls off a tomato, wipes it on his pants, puts it to his mouth to bite it. He can't bite it and realizes that it is made out of rubber. He throws it down, and the tomato bounces like a ball. He throws his crutch down and with a desperate move he pulls the entire bush out with both hands. As he pulls he falls on his back with the tomato bush on top of him. Instead of roots, the tomato bush has all kinds of electrical wiring. The light becomes dim. A mellow waltz is heard coming from the soldier's radio. A young couple and an elderly couple both dressed in formal clothes are dancing around the soldier still covered by the bush. Each couple has a tomato which they play with, passing it from beneath one partner's chin to the other. Noisy giggles of happiness. As the couples disappear the music stops. The soldier frees himself from the bush and jumps up at once towards his radio. He puts on his earphones and taps the radio, desperately screaming. His scream turns into crying: 'HELLO! HELLO! HELLO!' He collapses and falls asleep with his earphones on. The stage blackens.

The stage fills with morning light. He gets up, rubs his eyes, looks in amazement at the tomato bush with all the wires sticking out from the ground. As he tries to remove the tomato bush he is pulling more wires out from the ground until they are covering his parachute, his radio, his knapsack and his entire safety island. Suddenly he starts

Hinges

searching desperately for the radio, for his earphones, for his knapsack. He finds them, takes out of his knapsack a pair of pliers, cuts a wire from the tomato bush roots, connects it to his radio (all this with great excitement), puts on his earphones and the radio is working. He is screaming with joy. From the radio we hear, 'And now, ladies and gentlemen, we give you the latest news.' We see him falling on his knees on the wires, holding his radio with one hand and with the other beating his forehead in great horror as he looks upwards. He removes his earphones and as the radio is transmitting incoherently, he throws the radio towards the fields. As the radio is in mid-air, the stage darkens, and we hear an explosion.

Curtain

V
THE MYSTERY OF THE KINGFISHER BOX

George Moor

Photograph by courtesy of George Moor

George Moor has for some years taught English abroad, most notably in Saudi Arabia, Japan and Iran. His volume of short novels, *Fox Gold* has been published by John Calder (Publishers) Ltd and his short story 'The Heat of the Sun' appeared in *NWW* 13.

THE MYSTERY OF THE KINGFISHER BOX

Other books by the same author

The Heat of the Sun (in New Writing and Writers 13)

Fox Gold, Nightingale Island, Bowl of Roses (short stories)

In preparation

The Flute of Silence and *Bald Beauty* (two novels)